MICHAEL THE AMAZING
MIND-READING
SAUSAGE DOG

To Rex,
Stay pawesome!

For Sedwig, Bucky and Snoop

-TC

For Baxter, my very own wonder pup! x

-TB

MICHAEL THE AMAZING MIND-READING SAUSAGE DOG

By ~~Terrie Chilvers~~ *Michael*

Illustrated by ~~Tim Budgen~~ *Michael*

First published in 2023
by Firefly Press

25 Gabalfa Road, Llandaff North, Cardiff, CF14 2JJ
www.fireflypress.co.uk

A CIP catalogue record of this book is
available from the British Library.

1 3 5 7 9 8 6 4 2

Print ISBN 9781915444134
ebook ISBN 9781915444141

This book has been published with the support
of the Books Council of Wales.

Typeset and design
by Becka Moor

Printed and bound by CPI Group (UK) Ltd, Croydon, CR0 4YY

FSC
www.fsc.org
MIX
Paper | Supporting
responsible forestry
FSC® C171272

DEDICATION

THIS BOOK ABOUT ME IS
DEDICATED TO MY LOYAL FRIEND,
STANLEY BIG DOG. THANK YOU
FOR ALWAYS BELIEVING IN
JUST HOW FANTASTIC I AM
AND HELPING ME SHARE MY
OUTSTANDING NATURAL TALENT
WITH THE WORLD.

— MICHAEL

A NOTE FROM MICHAEL

Congratulations on your excellent choice of book. Of course, I already knew you were going to pick it up. You're in for a treat. This is the story of me, Michael the Amazing Mind-Reading Sausage Dog, and my rise to fame and fortune. You've probably already heard of me, or even been to one of my sell-out shows. But the road to stardom was no walkies in the park. It took blood, sweat, tears and a lot of doggie treats to get where I am today. Now the time has finally come to share my amazing journey with you.

Along the way I will reveal my secrets and give you a glimpse into the fascinating world of mind-reading – from the tiniest of terriers to the most gigantic of Great Danes. You may even find you can read minds yourself (but don't get too excited as it's a very rare talent). Prepare yourself for one of the greatest stories of our time. How one small hound became the most famous sausage dog in the world. Ever.

Michael

The Amazing Mind-Reading Sausage Dog

Chapter 1
A STAR IS BORN

My name is Michael the Amazing,
Mind-Reading, World-Famous Sausage
Dog Sensation. But you can just call me
Michael. Of course, I haven't always been a
superstar sausage dog who can read minds – I
was once an extremely ordinary dog.

To understand my epic rise to fame, we need to go back to the start when I was just a tiny sausage pup. My story begins in the small town of Snuffles-by-Sea. I lived by myself in a small house I'd inherited from my great aunt, Louisa Little Legs. There wasn't much going on in Snuffles for a dog with ambition. The most exciting thing was the Pork Chop Café in the park, and if you wanted to buy a decent waistcoat you had to go all the way to Little Paw!

The only Snuffles-by-Sea resident who had gone on to do anything interesting was Susan the Chocolate Labrador. Susan had won a local talent show by balancing peanuts on her nose. Balancing peanuts! I knew that my talent was far superior. I knew that my talent was amazing. I just had to work out exactly what it was.

And it didn't take me long…

I was taking a stroll in the park. There had just been a rain shower and I had opted for a striking yellow waterproof waistcoat and a fabulous yellow hat. Yes, I was looking adorable. I was having a splash around in my favourite puddle (the one next to the smallest pine tree) when I heard something…

This is the BEST STICK EVER. And it belongs to Stanley Big Dog. Nobody else!

I turned to see an extremely tall and very hairy dog. He had a large stick in his mouth and his eyes were darting around like he'd eaten way too many chicken chews.

How could I hear this dog's voice? His mouth was full of stick!

Uh oh. That sausage dog is looking at my stick! But this stick belongs to Stanley Big Dog. And nobody else!

My paws were tingling and my ears were twitching. Could I be ... reading this dog's mind?

'Stanley? Stanley Big Dog?' I said out loud. And Stanley's ears pricked up. His head tilted to one side, trying to work out how I could possibly know his name.

'Hello there, young sir, could I trouble you for just a minute?' I said, in my finest, important-sounding voice.

Stanley Big Dog looked at me for a few seconds, then turned ... and ran away!

I chased after him. Stanley Big Dog was my ticket to fame and fortune – I couldn't let him get away!

Some people say that sausage dogs are not the most athletic of breeds. They say that short, stubby legs and a body shaped like a sausage is not the best combination for running at speed through the park on a wet and windy day. But they have not met me.

On this particular day, I ran so fast that other dogs may have confused me with a greyhound. Unfortunately, I was so busy concentrating on running like the wind that I completely lost sight of Stanley Big Dog and was forced to abandon the chase.

This was a disaster! The first dog whose mind I could read, and I'd lost him forever! It was still raining so I sheltered under a large oak tree – I was getting wet despite my fabulous yellow waterproof waistcoat and hat.

But then, out of nowhere, my paws began to tingle and my ears began to twitch…

Everybody's always trying to take my stick. Nobody's getting THIS stick today! This stick belongs to Stanley Big Dog. And nobody else!

I peered round the oak tree, and there was Stanley Big Dog on the other side! He peered back at me with the same crazy eyes as before.

I was reading his mind! I could hardly believe my adorable, silky ears. I really had found my talent! I was a mind-reading sausage dog! I'd never heard of any dog reading minds – this was amazing. I was amazing! My talent was a million times better than balancing peanuts. I always knew it would be!

uh oh! That sausage dog is looking at my stick again.

Stanley cocked his head to one side and had a good look at me in my wet weather outfit.

This stick does not belong to a miniature sausage dog dressed like a sailor.

I looked down at my exquisite yellow raincoat with bright blue buttons and tiny blue tassels where it fastened around my neck. I was not going to stand for this insult to my fabulous clothing – even if it was Stanley's mind-voice and not his real voice. I marched round to the other side of the oak tree.

'I am a standard-sized sausage dog, thank you very much. And this outfit is way too sophisticated for a sailor!'

Stanley Big Dog's stick fell from his mouth. He was in complete shock.

'How do you know what I'm thinking? Only Stanley Big Dog can hear what Stanley Big Dog is thinking,' he said.

'That's why I've been chasing you!' I said. 'I've been trying to explain – I can read minds. Well, so far, only yours. But this is just the beginning! With practice I think I could read the mind of any dog!'

'And you don't want my stick?' said Stanley Big Dog.

I looked at the stick on the floor, covered in slobber, bits of leaf and clumps of Stanley's fur. 'No,' I said.

'Great!' said Stanley Big Dog. 'Let's be friends!'

This was very good news. And we hadn't even had to sniff each other's bums! I could practise my mind-reading on Stanley Big Dog and move one step closer to becoming the most talented dog in Snuffles-by-Sea!

Chapter 2
THE WRONG END OF THE STICK

Finally, I'd found my talent. Somehow, an extremely hairy dog I'd never seen before in my life had unlocked my amazing ability to read minds! Strange, but true! And now I had a friend to help me explore just how spectacular my talent was.

'Are you free tomorrow afternoon for some mind-reading practice?' I asked Stanley. 'You'll just need to think about lots of different things so I can read your mind. Preferably not sticks all the time. And then tell me if I'm getting it right. Which of course I will be, but a professional still needs to double check.'

Stanley wasn't listening; he was too busy scratching his bottom up against a knobbly old tree.

'Stanley! Can we practise tomorrow?' I barked, a little louder this time.

Stanley bounded over and I noticed something stuck to his bum.

'What's that?' I said.

'What?' asked Stanley.

'There's something stuck to your behind...' I said.

'Oh, that's just Stanley Big Dog's tail,' replied Stanley. 'It's always there!'

Stanley gave his tail a good wag to make his point.

'No, not that!' I said, shaking my head. 'There's something else. It must have been stuck on the tree.' I looked at the piece of paper stuck in Stanley's fur. It was a poster showing a familiar smug-looking chocolate Labrador balancing a peanut on her nose…

DO YOU HAVE A HIDDEN TALENT?

ARE YOU AN ORDINARY DOG WITH AN EXTRAORDINARY SKILL?

TALENTED DOGS OF SNUFFLES-BY-SEA – WE NEED YOU!

THE ANNUAL 'SEARCH FOR A SU-PAW-STAR' TALENT COMPETITION IS BACK!

THE GRAND PRIZE – YOUR WEIGHT IN WAGTASTIC BEEFY BITES & TURKEY TASTIES.

FEATURING SPECIAL GUEST JUDGE AND LAST YEAR'S WINNER, SUSAN THE CHOCOLATE LABRADOR!!!

(PLEASE BRING OWN PROPS – WE CANNOT PROVIDE GLITTER CANES OR SPARKLY MICROPHONES)

Surely this was written to me personally! I had a hidden talent! I was extraordinary! And I had my own personal glitter cane and sparkly microphone! This was the opportunity I needed – what better way to introduce my new-found talent to the dogs of Snuffles-by-Sea? Of course, I would have preferred a different guest judge from the super-annoying and overrated Susan the Chocolate Labrador, but you can't have everything.

'What is it?' said Stanley, trying to crane his head round to read the poster.

'There's a talent show and I'm going to win it!' I said.

Stanley's tail wagged. 'I've never been in a talent show before! Stanley will be great!'

'Oh, I think you've got the wrong end of the stick,' I replied. 'My act is more of a one dog performance.'

'What stick? My stick?' said Stanley, his head cocked to one side.

'No, it's just a saying…' I replied, but Stanley wasn't listening.

'Stanley Big Dog is going to be your assistant!' barked Stanley, running around in circles and looking like he'd just dug up the world's biggest bone.

Oh dear. I'd managed to get myself in quite a pickle. Having a big hairy sidekick wasn't part of my masterplan. And Stanley Big Dog definitely wouldn't have been my first choice as an assistant. But I needed to master the art of mind-reading, so I would just have to go along with it.

There was just one thing I needed to check…

'How do you feel about wearing a waistcoat for the performance?' I asked.

Stanley Big Dog raised a big hairy eyebrow.

'You'll love it!' I replied. 'I've got something FABULOUS in mind!'

Chapter 3
AN EXTREMELY HAIRY NEW
ASSISTANT

Stanley Big Dog and I had two days to prepare for the talent show that would change my life. But getting Stanley's attention for longer than five minutes was making mind-reading practice difficult. I'd promised Stanley a plate of pork chops if we worked on our act for the whole afternoon.

'OK, stand still so I can read your mind,' I said.

'What about my tail, Michael?' said Stanley, his tail wagging like it was trying to shake itself loose.

'It's OK, just keep the rest of you still,' I replied.

I tried to concentrate and waited, just like in the park. But all I could hear was the swishing of Stanley's tail.

'It's not working!' I said. 'I wonder why it's not working?'

Stanley was staring into space.

'What were you thinking about?' I asked Stanley.

'Nothing, Michael,' replied Stanley.

'What do you mean?' I said.

'You didn't tell me to think of anything. I was just concentrating on standing still,' said Stanley.

I took a deep breath. Working with Stanley Big Dog was going to be tough … but at least he was trying. And right now, he was the only way I was going to become an expert mind-reader and win the talent show.

'OK, can you think of something this time?' I asked.

Stanley looked thoughtful and gave his ear a bit of a scratch. 'What shall I think about, Michael?'

'Stanley! I can't tell you what to think about. Then we won't know if I'm reading your mind or not!' I said.

'Right, right!' said Stanley. 'OK, I'm doing it now.'

Stanley stood very still (apart from his very waggy tail) and was concentrating so hard I thought his eyes might pop out of his big, hairy head.

I closed my eyes and tried to focus.

And then it happened…

My paws began to tingle.

And my ears began to twitch.

Stanley Big Dog's mind-voice was coming through loud and clear!

I wish Michael would hurry up. I'm desperate for a wee and that plate of pork chops Michael promised me. I wonder how many pork chops there will be?

I ran around in circles. 'It's working! I'm reading your mind, Stanley!'

Stanley started running around in circles with me.

'You're thinking about needing a wee and eating pork chops!' I barked.

'That's right!' said Stanley, suddenly stopping and having a quick wee at the foot of a tree.

'And now you're just thinking about pork chops,' I replied.

I was doing it! I'd harnessed my powers! Reading Stanley's mind in the park hadn't been a one-off – I had the kind of talent that could shake the world to its very core!

Once I had mastered the art of reading Stanley's mind, I found I could read the mind of ANY DOG! The poodle next door, a greyhound in the park, the French Bulldog waiter at the Pork Chop Café ... anyone! I just had to stand near to my subject, close my eyes and wait for my paws to tingle and my ears to twitch. I found that wearing a fabulous waistcoat also helped quite a lot.

Stanley Big Dog and I rehearsed our act for the talent show from dusk until dawn, with pork-chop breaks for Stanley, of course. And by the time the talent show rolled round, we were ready to show the residents of Snuffles-By-Sea just how talented I was!

Chapter 4
THE GRAND FANCY THEATRE ROYALE

Stanley Big Dog and I arrived at the talent show venue raring to go. We were wearing matching gold-sequinned waistcoats. Unfortunately, Stanley's was a couple of sizes too small, but that didn't matter! A fabulous waistcoat can make any dog look a million dollars.

The talent show was being held at the Grand Fancy Theatre Royale in the Snuffles-by-Sea town centre. But when Stanley and I trotted into the entrance hall, we were greeted by a theatre that was far from grand and fancy.

There was paint peeling off the walls and the organisers of the show had laid out a grubby red carpet for the entrants. The carpet looked like it hadn't been washed for years and smelt of wet dogs and meat breath. Within seconds Stanley was rolling around on it with his paws in the air.

'Stanley! Be professional!' I said. 'You'll ruin your waistcoat! There will be plenty of time for that later when we're celebrating our big win!'

'Sorry, Michael,' said Stanley, managing to squeeze in one final wiggle.

I spotted a disapproving Yorkshire Terrier at the other end of the red carpet who seemed to be in charge. She was wearing a headset to communicate with the crew backstage. Clearly all the budget had been spent on that headset because the rest of the show looked extremely ramshackle! I took a deep breath. If I wanted to become world-famous, I had to start at the bottom.

'Come on, Stanley,' I barked, and we bounded over towards our destiny. Well, I bounded, Stanley Big Dog lolloped.

'Next!' barked the Yorkshire Terrier.

'Lovely to meet you … Mandy!' I said, reading the tag on her collar. 'What a fantastic theatre this is!'

'Name, please,' said Mandy, studying her clipboard.

'Michael the Mind-Reading Sausage Dog,' I replied, bowing at the end for flair.

Stanley stopped scratching himself for a brief second and looked at me.

'Oh, and Stanley Big Dog, my assistant,' I added.

Mandy the Yorkshire Terrier finally looked up and eyeballed me.

'You're too short,' she yapped. 'Nobody will be able to see you on the stage. You have to be taller than that…' she said, pointing at a life-sized cut-out of a medium-sized dog standing next to a measuring stick.

My heart sunk. I was not a medium-sized dog; I was a small-sized dog.

'It's in the rules,' she said, tapping her clipboard and looking around like she was trying to spot some medium-sized dogs.

'Then I'll need to speak to the manager!' I replied. 'This is unacceptable!'

'The manager's having her lunch. And we're under strict instructions not to disturb her,' said Mandy.

'But I have an act that will truly wow people. It doesn't matter about my size!' I said.

Mandy frowned and looked at my short, furry legs. 'Can you wear stilts?'

'I'm a mind-reader, not a clown!' I barked.

Mandy glanced over at Stanley Big Dog. 'He can enter. He's PLENTY big enough.'

'Stanley?' I said. Stanley was now licking a part of himself that I can't really mention here. Somehow, I didn't think the residents of Snuffles-by-Sea would be interested in watching Stanley Big Dog do THAT for five minutes… 'We only perform together,' I replied.

'Well then, the show will just have to go on without you,' snorted Mandy.

Stanley Big Dog gave me a friendly nudge with his snout. 'Maybe next year, Michael. When you're bigger.'

'Stanley! This is my full size! I'm not going to get any bigger,' I said.

This was a disaster! How was I going to be a world-famous mind-reading sausage dog if I couldn't even perform at the local talent competition? I had to make this happen.

I puffed out my chest. 'Of course, if you were able to help us out now, I'd be able to get you front row tickets at my show in the future,' I said.

'But you're not famous yet,' said Mandy.

'No, but I will be. It's just a matter of time,' I replied.

Mandy's headset crackled. She was getting a message from backstage.

'What do you mean Elsbeth has lost her voice?' said Mandy.

My ears pricked up.

'But she's our best act!' barked Mandy. 'She was supposed to be singing "I Will Always Woof You" by Whippety Houston! Now we've only got three entrants! We can't hold a talent show with three entrants. We need at least four!'

I stepped forward and tried to look taller than I was. Mandy turned away.

'This is terrible!' said Mandy into her headset. 'Mayoress Benjamina Bulldog is coming to watch the show! What are we going to do?!'

Stanley was back to licking himself.

'Stanley, try to look presentable!' I whispered. 'We might have a chance of getting on the show!'

I shuffled round into Mandy's line of sight, dragging Stanley with me.

Mandy eyeballed us, then scanned the entrance hall for any other options. But fortunately for Stanley and me there was only a potted plant and half a box of discarded turkey giblet popcorn. She seemed to give some serious thought to the potted plant.

'OK, you're in,' she said, looking at my legs again. 'You'll have to stand on a chair or something.'

'Not a problem,' I said. Because I knew that I could be a star no matter what I was standing on. I could be sitting on a cow pat and still shine. Stanley Big Dog and I walked through to the dressing room. My journey was just beginning. Today Snuffles-by-Sea, tomorrow my very own sell-out show in Hollywoof!

Chapter 5
THIS IS MY MOMENT!

The 'Search for a Su-paw-star' talent competition was in full swing. Clyde the Rockstar Chihuahua had gone down a storm and a poodle dance troupe was currently on stage doing a jazz routine. Stanley and I would be the last act to perform and I actually felt a little bit nervous as I waited in the wings. I asked myself these questions:

Are you talented enough, Michael?

Can you really do this, Michael?

Do you have what it takes to be a mind-reading sausage dog sensation and wow this audience beyond their wildest dreams, Michael?

And then I answered myself with a resounding YES! Of course you can do this Michael, because you're fantastic!

Head judge, and last year's Su-paw-star winner, Susan the Chocolate Labrador took to the stage after the poodle dancers.

'Thank you to the Waggington Jazz Poodles! Let's give them a round of apawse and some tail wags!' said Susan.

I took a deep breath. It was nearly my moment.

'And next, I'd like to introduce our final act...' announced Susan. 'Michael the Mind-Reading Sausage Dog!'

I strutted onto the stage to greet my adoring public. They didn't know they adored me yet, but they would soon. I took centre stage.

'Welcome to *Search for a Su-paw-star!*' said Susan, who was now sitting behind the judge's table in front of the stage.

I should mention, to avoid future disappointment, that Susan the Chocolate Labrador is not MADE of chocolate as her name would suggest. She's just boringly the COLOUR of chocolate. And of course, her talent is just as boring. We would all balance peanuts on our noses if we had nothing better to do. You're probably balancing two on your nose right now. And if you are, I'm not going to congratulate you, because it is NOT a talent.

'We're really excited to see what you've got!' continued Susan. 'The stage is all yours!'

That's what Susan said ... but I had a strong feeling that Susan was poised and ready to relive last year's glory at the slightest opportunity. There was a glint in her eye and a bag of peanuts under the table.

Sitting next to Susan at the judging table was the other judge, a Great Dane called Giles. He was wearing a silk scarf and looked like he'd been made to smell a bag of mouldy pork chops. Stanley and I would have to impress them both if we wanted to win the show.

I took a deep breath and tried to block out the sound of Stanley Big Dog panting off stage. He'd spent most of our time in the dressing room chasing his own tail and was now completely exhausted. I held my snout high and began...

'Good evening, ladies and gentledogs! My name is Michael the Mind-Reading Sausage Dog and you're about to witness something spectacular! I am gifted with an extraordinary and unique talent, and today I am sharing it with you. One extremely lucky dog in the audience is about to get their mind read by ME!'

The audience gasped. Tails wagged. One large dog's tail was wagging so excitedly it knocked a miniature poodle right off her seat.

'I will now invite my assistant to the stage, please welcome … Mr Stanley Big Dog!' I boomed, and I held my tiny glitter cane out to one side to the exact spot where Stanley should have been standing. But there was no Stanley.

'Mr Stanley Big Dog!' I repeated. The audience was now completely silent. But then there was a small snort from someone in the front row, and soon the whole audience was yapping with laughter. I turned around and was horrified to see Stanley on the other side of the stage, furiously trying to eat a toffee that was stuck between two floorboards.

'Stanley!' I hissed. 'Leave the toffee! This is the most important day of our lives!'

Stanley didn't respond, but I was close enough to hear his thoughts loud and clear…

Toffee! This is Stanley Big Dog's toffee! And nobody else's!

Oh no. Not this again. Whenever Stanley wanted something, he REALLY wanted something.

Toffee! This is Stanley's toffee! said Stanley's mind-voice.

Susan and Giles looked confused. They were probably wondering if this was part of the act. It wasn't. Stanley and I had practised our performance for hours in the park. And not once had it involved furiously digging for a toffee with slobber flying everywhere.

'Can you hurry this along, please,' said Giles. 'We haven't got all day. Some of us have afternoon naps curled up by the fire scheduled.'

'Let's not rush them,' said Susan. 'They're clearly just having some ... technical difficulties. And of course, if absolutely necessary, I can always entertain the audience in the meantime!'

I could see Susan reaching for the peanuts under her desk.

'Stanley!' I barked. But it was no use. Stanley was in a TOTAL TOFFEE TRANCE. There was only one thing for it ... Stanley had to be united with the toffee.

I ran over and pawed at the sweet, desperately trying to release it from the floorboards. But the toffee was stuck fast. I felt sick. My dreams were slipping away. Every minute spent trying to get Stanley's stupid toffee was a minute not wowing the audience with my mind-reading act! But then the sparkle of my glitter cane caught my eye. I grabbed it and crammed it between the floorboards. I could lever out the toffee!

I was almost there, and with one almighty flick, the toffee was free! The show could go on! Well, that would have been the case ... if I hadn't flicked it in the worst possible direction.

The toffee flew through the air, over the head of Stanley Big Dog and straight towards the judge's table! I watched it soar ... and land right on Susan's head, where it stuck like a very small, weird hat.

Could things get any worse?

Yes.

Stanley Big Dog bounded after the toffee, leapt onto the judge's table and gobbled it right off the top of Susan's head. Then he casually trotted back to the stage.

I was horrified. Things were going terribly and I hadn't even started my act yet!

The audience were silent and there were no more tails wagging.

Giles was gobsmacked. And Susan was lost for words. But not for long.

She turned to the audience and shook the slobber from her head. 'Maybe I should start balancing toffees on my head instead of peanuts on my nose?'

The audience cheered.

I couldn't believe it. This was supposed to be my moment, but instead of wowing the audience, I was helping Susan the Chocolate Labrador build her fanbase!

'Stanley!' I barked.

'Oh. Hi … Michael…' said Stanley Big Dog, licking his lips. 'Is it time for the act now?'

'Yes, Stanley. Yes, it is,' I said, with my superstar smile plastered on my superstar face. Now was not the time to be angry with Stanley

Big Dog. There was still time to shine. Maybe, just maybe I could carry on as if nothing had happened.

I turned to the audience. 'As I was saying, I will need a volunteer...'

There was a small hum of activity. The audience clearly weren't used to being in the presence of a real superstar. Eventually they got used to the idea and two dogs put up their paws. I selected a young dappled greyhound sitting in the front row. Stanley Big Dog fetched the greyhound onto the stage. We were back on track!

'What's your name?' I asked.

'Gary. Gary the Greyhound,' said Gary the Greyhound.

'Please write your favourite food on the card provided by Stanley Big Dog,' I said. 'And then think about that food, and only that food.'

I put on my glittery blindfold and prepared myself for dazzling the audience with my talent.

I heard the squeak of the marker pen as Gary wrote down his favourite food. I concentrated hard and tuned into Gary's mind-voice.

I paused to ramp up the tension.

'Roast chicken!' I announced.

I was certain that Gary was thinking about roast chicken. Every bone in my sausage body and every strand of my fur knew that Gary was thinking about roast chicken. I waited for the audience to cheer.

'Erm, that's not it,' said Gary.

I couldn't believe my ears. This had never happened in practice.

The audience gasped, and not in a good way. I peeked over the top of my blindfold.

Giles the judge looked horrified at my apparent lack of talent, and Susan's paw was back on her bag of peanuts ready to steal the limelight.

'Let me try that again!' I quickly announced.

I took a deep breath. It wasn't over yet, but if I got this wrong, I would be doomed to a life of normality, and that would mean:

- **No sell-out tour in Hollywoof**

- **No fans asking for my pawtograph**

- **No dogs wearing my new line of fabulous waistcoats**

Everything rested on this moment...

Chapter 6
A PESKY PUG CALLED PRISCILLA

So there I was, standing in the middle of the stage trying to read Gary the Greyhound's mind. I still had my glittery blindfold on so I couldn't see a thing, but I'm pretty sure the audience and judges were open-mouthed, waiting to see if I could overcome this setback and win the talent show.

I felt a tingle in my paws. I could do this.

'I've got it!' I cried. The audience fell silent, most likely teetering on the edge of their seats.

'Your favourite food isn't just roast chicken

… it's roast chicken smothered in strawberry ice cream!'

I whipped off the blindfold. This time I was certain I'd got it right.

Gary the Greyhound was licking his lips like he hadn't eaten for a week. 'Yes, yes!' he barked. 'That's it! Roast chicken and strawberry ice cream – the most delicious meal on Earth!'

Stanley Big Dog revealed the answer on the board and the crowd went wild. I punched the air with one superstar paw and then began a series of superstar bows. I was entertainment gold! I even spotted grumpy Giles the judge wagging his tail!

There were no more acts left and it was obvious that I was the best! I was clearly going to win and then I'd be one step closer to becoming the most famous sausage dog in the world. Ever!

Susan looked a bit nervous. There was a new talent in town! She wouldn't be needing those peanuts today!

But I was rudely interrupted by a shout from the back of the theatre. 'He's a fake. I bet Gary's his brother and this is all planned!'

I snorted. 'That's ridiculous! And anyway, Gary's a greyhound and I'm a sausage dog! It's genetically impossible for us to be brothers!'

'Prove it!' said the heckler, as they walked down the aisle towards the stage. A small wrinkly pug appeared from the shadows. 'Read MY mind!' she said, barging to the front of the theatre and onto the stage.

I was so shocked I couldn't speak, which is extremely rare for me.

'My name is Priscilla,' said the intruder, turning to the audience. 'And I believe this miniature sausage dog is a fake!'

'I'm not a miniature sausage dog! I'm a standard-sized sausage dog!' I replied, trying to stay calm.

But nobody cared. Everyone was much more interested in whether Priscilla the Pug was about to reveal me as a fraudster. The very thought! I was a genuine talent!

Priscilla snatched the answer board from a stunned Stanley Big Dog and starting furiously writing. 'If you really can read minds, read mine and tell everyone what my middle name is,' she barked.

I had never seen a pug look so smug.

But I was not concerned because I was born

for moments like these! I closed my eyes, concentrated and waited for my paws to tingle and my ears to twitch. But there was nothing. Not even a tiny tingle. At this point I would normally hear the subject's mind-voice, but weirdly Priscilla's mind-voice sounded like a squeaky toy in a washing machine and I couldn't understand a word. I couldn't believe it! This had never happened with any of the dogs I'd practised on!

Susan and Giles were whispering to each other behind the judges' table. The audience was getting impatient, and some dogs were even starting to leave.

'He's rubbish!' barked a Bernese Mountain Dog.

'Michael the Scamming Sausage Dog more like it!' said a disgruntled Dalmatian in the front row.

'It's true, the greyhound must be his brother!' cried a Chihuahua.

Even Gary the Greyhound seemed to be considering the idea that he might actually be my brother and was somehow part of a major scam that he'd organised without even knowing about it.

Susan the Chocolate Labrador rushed up onto the stage. 'Quiet!' she barked. 'Sit! SIT!'

All the dogs in the audience stopped yapping and sat down.

'Show us some acts with real talent!' grumbled the disgruntled Dalmatian under his breath.

'Well, I suppose there might be time for a peanut trick at the end,' she paused. 'If that's what the residents of Snuffles-by-Sea want, of course.'

Annoyingly, it was exactly what the residents of Snuffles-by-Sea wanted, and they all started chanting Susan's name.

'OK, OK! But first let's announce this year's winner,' she said.

Priscilla the Pug scuttled off back to her seat, but the damage was done.

Susan continued, 'Thank you so much for your performance, Michael and Stanley. It was certainly ... entertaining! Now, could all the contestants please make their way back onto the stage.'

All of the contestants trotted back onto the stage. I could barely look at them – I had more talent in my left ear than all of them put together!

There was a drum roll as Susan began to announce the winner. 'And the paws down winner is…'

Susan waited for what seemed like a lifetime. I knew I'd lost; I didn't even have to read Susan's mind to know that. I couldn't bear it. I deserved to win! Stanley Big Dog's tail was wagging. He clearly thought we still had a chance.

And then Susan finally crushed our dreams.

'The winner is … Clyde the Rockstar Chihuahua!' she barked.

I tried not to look devastated. But it was hard. There was a shiny trophy overflowing with tasty bones for the winner. And a Pomeranian photographer appeared from nowhere to take pictures of Clyde headbanging with Susan. Clyde would be on the front page of the *Daily Woof* newspaper tomorrow.

And me and Stanley Big Dog? We finished joint last. With the jazz poodles!

All in all, it had been a disastrous start to my new mind-reading career. Not only had we lost the talent show, I couldn't stop thinking about what had happened with the pug. Why couldn't I read Priscilla's mind? I thought I could read the mind of any dog, but now I wasn't so sure...

Chapter 7
IMPORTANT BUSINESS AT THE
PORK CHOP CAFÉ

My dream was over. After the absolute disaster at the talent show, Clyde the Rockstar Chihuahua was getting invited to all the best events. One day he'd be guest of honour at a tail chasing in Little Paw...

...And the next he would be unveiling a statue of a giant pork chop in the park. Not that I was following his schedule extremely closely. Of course, Susan was getting in on the act too, and the two of them would often appear as a pair at extra special events.

I spent a whole week wallowing in my basket under a fleecy blanket. I didn't even have the energy to put on a fabulous waistcoat. I hadn't attempted any mind-reading since Priscilla the Pug, and probably never would again. My dream was over. Well, that was what I thought until Stanley Big Dog arrived one afternoon with a big slobbery stick and a spring in his step.

'This is definitely the best stick,' said Stanley, dropping it next to me. 'And I've only chewed one end of it, so it's extra special.'

This had been our routine for the last seven days. Stanley would bring a stick to try to cheer me up, then I would mutter a thank-you but would still feel the same. I was a failure. It was like the fire inside me had gone out, like I was a rubber toy with a broken squeaker.

I slowly lifted my head to look at today's stick. It was the biggest yet. Stanley's tail was wagging, still hopeful that a knobbly piece of tree could fix everything and get me back on track.

'You don't have to keep bringing me sticks, Stanley. I'm fine,' I said, curling up into a ball and closing my eyes.

But then my paws began to tingle and my ears began to twitch…

Tomorrow's stick will be even better! It will be bigger! And knobblier! Maybe I'll bring two!

I opened one eye and saw Stanley staring at all the rejected sticks piled up in the corner. He wasn't downhearted. In fact, Stanley's tail was wagging even more crazily than usual. My other eye sprung open as the truth hit me!

Stanley wasn't put off by the big pile of sticks. He didn't see failure – he saw an opportunity to try again tomorrow!

'Stanley Big Dog – you're a genius!' I barked, leaping out of my basket.

'I don't think so, Michael. I was bottom of the class at puppy school,' replied Stanley.

'I can't give up now! We have to try again! We must! After all, the world deserves to see my talent,' I said, holding my snout high for the first time in days.

Stanley's tail wagged. Not that it had ever stopped.

The very next morning I arranged a business meeting with Stanley Big Dog. We met at the Pork Chop Café to discuss our next move. I ordered a puppaccino for me and three crispy pork chops with a side of chicken chews for Stanley Big Dog. I didn't have to ask Stanley what he wanted any more. We'd spent so much time together practising our act that I could read his mind much more quickly than I could other dogs. Although to be honest, I didn't really have to bother because he always wanted three crispy pork chops and a side of chicken chews.

'We need to come up with a plan,' I said to Stanley.

'A plan for what?' said Stanley, sniffing the air to smell if his food was on the way.

'A plan for becoming famous, of course!' I replied.

'Can we do it after the pork chops?' said Stanley.

'This is important business, Stanley. Time does not stand still for pork chops!' I replied. 'The talent show was a disaster and now we need to win back the public. We need to come back stronger and more talented than ever before. We'll be more famous than Clyde. More famous than Susan. And most importantly...'

'Did somebody order pork chops?' barked the French Bulldog waiter.

'Yes, please!' said Stanley, and he started tucking in like they were the only pork chops left on the planet.

I tried to block out the sound of Stanley's chewing and carried on regardless. 'If we want to make it in Hollywoof, we need to find a dog that will put in a good word for us. Do we know any dogs with American relatives?'

'Don't think so,' said Stanley, spraying bits of pork chop everywhere.

Being famous in Snuffles-by-Sea was one thing, but having a show in Hollywoof was on a whole other level. Only true su-paw-stars made it there, and the real top dogs got their pawprint on the Hollywoof Walk of Fame. Hollywoof was where we needed to be.

'Maybe we could just go to Hollywoof and see what happens,' I suggested, fishing half a pork chop out of my puppaccino. 'But we don't have enough money for tickets.'

I gave my ear a good scratch to help me think. 'And we definitely don't know any dogs who live in Hollywoof?' I asked.

Stanley swallowed down the last pork chop and looked thoughtful. 'Are there any more pork chops?'

We were interrupted by the tinkle of the bell on the café door as a new customer entered.

'Stanley!' barked the dog, so loudly that the entire café looked up from their plates.

Stanley's tail started wagging furiously as the huge hairy dog, even bigger than Stanley, bounded towards us.

'Nephew! How are you, pup? I spotted you through the window!' said the gigantic dog.

'Uncle Humphrey!' barked Stanley, and the two of them chased each other around in circles for a good few minutes. Eventually they came to a standstill.

'How rude of me!' said Humphrey, out of breath. 'I haven't said hello to your friend.'

'Hello,' I said. 'I'm Michael, pleased to meet you. Stanley and I work together.'

Pork Chop Café

'Humphrey Huge Dog, pleasure to meet you, chap,' he replied. 'I'm Stanley's uncle, visiting from overseas to see the family!'

'Can we get you a puppaccino?' I said, unsure if they would have a large enough puppaccino cup for Humphrey.

'No thanks, boys!' replied Humphrey. 'Just dropped in for a bag of pork chops. They don't make them like this in Hollywoof!'

I couldn't believe what I was hearing.

'You live in Hollywoof?' I said, almost choking on my drink.

'Sure do!' said Humphrey. 'Surprised Stanley didn't mention it! I'm the globetrotter of the family!'

'No, Stanley absolutely didn't mention it,' I said, glaring at Stanley.

'What?' replied Stanley, completely unaware that he'd been sitting on our secret weapon this whole time.

'Your uncle might know someone...' I muttered to Stanley under my breath. 'You know, someone who can help us get a spot on a Hollywoof show?'

'Oh, Uncle Humphrey is a business dog. He won't know anyone in the theatres!' barked Stanley loudly.

'Ah, the business of show!' said Humphrey Huge Dog, staring off into the distance. 'You can't beat working in show business! I wouldn't want to do anything else!'

Stanley looked none the wiser.

'I track down new talent for a little showcase of dogs in the Hollywoof Theatre...'

'*The Canine Spectacular*?' I asked, completely gobsmacked. I had dreamt of performing in *The Canine Spectacular* for most of my life – it was the longest-running, most fantastic theatre dog show in America. No, the world!

'Yes! That's the one!' chipped in Stanley, who rather unhelpfully now seemed to know everything about his extremely useful uncle.

I gritted my teeth. Stanley was quite possibly the most annoying assistant in the world. Humphrey Huge Dog was our ticket to Hollywoof and me becoming the most famous sausage dog in the world. Ever!

I took a deep breath and stood up on the tips of my paws to look more important. 'Actually Humphrey, myself and Stanley are performers! We're quite new to the scene, but we're very ambitious! Perhaps...'

'Sorry, chaps, can't stop to chat,' interrupted Humphrey. 'On my way to meet a very talented chocolate Labrador! I've got a very busy schedule today!'

'Of course, of course. We're pretty busy too!' I replied, nodding my head vigorously.

'Are we?' said Stanley.

'Yes! We're always busy!' I replied.

'Are you boys going to the Digging Championship over in Little Paw tomorrow?' asked Humphrey. 'Maybe we can talk some more there?'

'Definitely! The Little Paw Annual Hole Digging Championship is my favourite event of the year!' I replied.

'But Michael, you said it was a pile of old nonsense and you wouldn't go if some dog paid you,' said Stanley, unhelpfully.

'I'm sure I didn't! I was probably talking about the Snuffles Corgi Choir Championship. The Hole Digging Championship is completely different! I can't get enough of watching dogs dig holes!' I said, trying to sound believable.

'Fantastic!' said Humphrey, who was too busy grabbing a bag of takeaway pork chops to listen properly. 'See you tomorrow, boys!'

I ordered another puppaccino (with extra bacon sprinkles) to celebrate. We were on our way to Hollywoof! Well, just as soon as we persuaded Humphrey Huge Dog that *The Canine Spectacular* was in need of a world-class mind-reading sausage dog and his extremely annoying assistant.

Chapter 8
THE LITTLE PAW ANNUAL HOLE DIGGING CHAMPIONSHIP

The Little Paw Annual Hole Digging Championship attracted dogs from miles around. By the time Stanley and I arrived, it was in full swing and dirt was flying everywhere.

'Let's dig a hole!' said Stanley.

'There's no time for digging,' I said. 'We need to find Humphrey and persuade him to give us a slot on the *Hollywoof Canine Spectacular*.'

There was a stage set up for the prizes later, so I climbed up to get a better view of the park.

I spotted Humphrey over at the water bowl stand.

'Humphrey!' I said, rushing over. 'Great to bump into you!'

'Michael!' barked Humphrey Huge Dog. 'Lovely day for watching dogs dig holes!'

I tried to look enthusiastic but, honestly, with all the mud flying everywhere, I was more concerned about keeping my new floral waistcoat clean.

'I wanted to tell you about our act!' I said. I looked over to Stanley but ... he'd disappeared! I'd have to deal with our career development single-pawedly.

But Humphrey was distracted by something over my left shoulder. I turned to see Susan the Chocolate Labrador, heading into the VIP area.

'Susan is such a talent,' said Humphrey. 'And

so humble! I'm a big fan of the classic dog talents – peanut balancing, jumping, digging.'

My paws were sinking into the soft dirt, but I had to stand my ground. 'True, but there are also some great new acts around,' I said. 'For example, Stanley and I are…'

Humphrey gazed off into the distance again. 'Peanut balancing! Such a noble art! Forget your new-fangled acts – I overheard someone in the Pork Chop Café talking about a mind-reading dog and his assistant! How ridiculous! Can you believe it?'

My heart sunk. And before I could reply, Nigel, a tiny Pomeranian ball of fluff with a large megaphone, rushed over.

'Mr Humphrey, it's time to judge the holes! Follow me, please!' said Nigel.

And I waved goodbye to Humphrey and my dreams of appearing on the *Hollywoof Canine*

Spectacular. What now? I needed to find Stanley to discuss our next move.

There was no sign of him. But I did spot Clyde the Rockstar Chihuahua over by the stage. He was performing at the prize-giving ceremony. Maybe he could give me some tips on breaking into the industry.

'Clyde! Fancy bumping into you!' I said, trotting over. 'How's things?'

'Busy, bro!' replied Clyde, who looked a bit worse for wear. 'Late night at the premiere of *My Stick's Bigger Than Your Stick*. Great film! Even better after party!'

'Are you OK? You look tired,' I said, giving Clyde a sniff. He looked like he was still wearing last night's leather jacket.

'Yeah, I'll be fine, bro,' replied Clyde. 'I'm used to it. Last week I performed every night of the week! I haven't slept for days!' he said, leaning against a tree beside the stage.

'Is that wise?' I asked. 'I find sleep is fairly essential.'

'Rockstars don't need sleep!' replied Clyde.

At which point, Clyde slid down the tree and fell fast asleep. He curled up into a tight furry ball and let out a snuffly snore.

I gave him a little nudge with my snout. 'Clyde? Clyde?'

But there was no response. Just more snoring. Well, hopefully he would wake up before his performance at the prize-giving...

'Ladies and Gentledogs! Welcome to the Little Paw Hole Digging Championship!' barked the mayoress.

The crowd howled with excitement – Mayoress Benjamina Bulldog was already up on the stage!

'Before we announce the winners, I'd like to welcome our special guest, Clyde the Rockstar Chihuahua!' said the mayoress.

The crowd of digging dogs barked their appreciation and the mayoress turned to the side of the stage, waiting for Clyde.

I frantically prodded Clyde with my paw. 'Clyde! Clyde! You're on!'

But Clyde was still fast asleep and the more I shook Clyde, the more firmly asleep he seemed to be. His legs pedalled back and forth as though he was chasing squirrels in his dreams.

'Welcome, Clyde!' repeated the mayoress, more loudly this time.

There was only one thing for it. This audience needed entertaining, and if Clyde wasn't up to it, I knew a dog who was. Me!

I scrambled onto the stage.

'Where's Clyde?' whispered Mayoress Benjamina.

'Clyde can't perform,' I whispered. 'But I think I can help!'

The mayoress looked concerned. 'How can you possibly help?' she whispered. 'Aren't you the miniature sausage dog from the talent show that can't read minds?'

'No! I mean, yes! I'm the standard-sized sausage dog that CAN read minds!' I replied. And I whispered my plan into her ear.

The mayoress turned to the audience – they were losing interest. Some of the dogs had even started digging new holes.

'OK, I guess we don't have much choice,' she

said, before turning to the audience. 'Ladies and Gentledogs! We have a slight change to the entertainment!'

I spotted Humphrey in the audience. This was my chance to impress him! If he wouldn't listen to me explain my talent, I would just have to show him!

Chapter 9
THE MASSIVE SAUSAGE FIASCO

The mayoress stepped to the front of the stage and one of her Pomeranian assistants rushed on to hand me a microphone.

'As an extra special treat, Michael the Mind-Reading Sausage Dog will give the official welcome speech...' barked the mayoress, 'by reading my mind!'

I gave a little bow to the crowd.

The mayoress plopped herself down on the purple velvet cushion she carried everywhere, and the crowd fell silent.

There was still no sign of Stanley. Where on earth could he be? Luckily, I didn't need his blindfold and chalkboard today.

'OK, Michael, read my mind!' said the mayoress. She screwed up her face with such concentration that she gave herself even more wrinkles than a usual bulldog.

'I will now read the mayoress' mind,' I said, taking a step forward. I closed my eyes as I concentrated and felt the familiar tingle in my paws. I could hear exactly what the mayoress was thinking, and began to share it with the audience, word for word.

'Welcome everyone!' I declared. 'We are extremely proud to host the Little Paw Annual Hole Digging Championship!'

'That's amazing!' said the mayoress. 'That's exactly what I'm thinking!'

The audience suddenly perked up and all eyes were on me.

'Carry on, Michael!' barked the mayoress.

Now fully in the mind-reading zone, I continued. 'Thank you all for coming. Now let's get a move on so I can go home and eat some pork chops.'

'What?' said the mayoress, leaping up from her velvet cushion. 'That's not what I'm thinking! Most definitely not.' At which point, her stomach rumbled like an angry lion.

The crowd howled with laughter.

'Try again,' said the mayoress, sitting back down.

This was not going well. I was supposed to be wowing the audience, not making them laugh and offending Mayoress Benjamina!

I closed my eyes and concentrated. I could hear the mayoress' mind-voice as clear as a squeaky toy.

'It's lovely to see so many of you here for this

important occasion,' I said. 'Though I wish some of you hadn't bothered – most of these holes are a joke. I could do better with one paw and my eyes closed!'

The crowd fell silent.

'And such a scruffy bunch of entrants this year!' I continued. 'Every single one of you!'

'Right, right! That's enough of that! Time to announce the winner!' said the mayoress.

There was no round of apawse. Every single dog looked annoyed. Apart from Humphrey Huge Dog. He was in the front row chuckling to himself. Humphrey clearly thought my talent was a joke. This was even worse than the Snuffles-By-Sea talent show catastrophe!

I retreated to the back of the stage as Mayoress Benjamina composed herself and addressed the audience. 'With a hole that our judges described as "really deep and expertly dug", the winner is … Mr Pickles, a springer spaniel from Barksville! Come up and join us!'

Mr Pickles sprung up onto the stage, caked in mud and very excited.

'Congratulations, Mr Pickles!' said the mayoress. 'You walk away with the title of "Best Hole Digger of the Year" AND a string of gourmet sausages made from the rarest pork this side of Waggington East. Only one string of these special succulent sausages exists!'

A glob of drool dripped from Mr Pickles' mouth.

'Bring on the sausages!' said the mayoress.

The crowd barked with joy as Nigel and the rest of the Pomeranian crew wheeled in the trolley of sausages. But when the trolley reached the side of the stage, there was a huge CRAASSSH! And the sausages disappeared down a massive hole!

'The sausages!' gasped the mayoress. 'Who

would dig a hole so close to the stage!'

I knew exactly who would do something like that…

I rushed over to the side of the stage with Mayoress Benjamina. As I peered down the hole, my paws began to tingle and my ears began to twitch. I heard a familiar voice.

Ooh! Sausages from the sky! This is the best day ever!

Stanley Big Dog was tangled up at the bottom of the hole with Nigel the Pomeranian and a string of extremely rare sausages.

'Stanley, whatever you do, don't eat those sausages!' I barked. 'You need to bring them up here!'

'Can't I have just one?' asked an extremely waggy-tailed Stanley. He clambered out of the hole, dropping Nigel and the dirty sausages on the floor.

'Oh my!' said Mayoress Benjamina, staring at Stanley, Nigel and the sausages, all covered in dirt. The entire audience gathered to witness the great sausage fiasco.

'What have you done to the grand prize?' barked the mayoress.

'I'm really sorry,' said Stanley, with one hungry eye still on the sausages.

'I'm sure the sausages will be fine, they're just a little bit ... soiled,' I said. 'And only a small bit trampled on.'

'This is a complete disgrace!' said the horrified mayoress. 'Never in the history of the Little Paw Annual Hole Digging Championship have I witnessed such chaos!'

'I've found a good one!' barked Stanley, holding aloft a muddy sausage.

Mayoress Benjamina shook her head.

'I declare this year's Annual Hole Digging Championship over!' she barked. 'Nigel, make sure Mr Pickles gets a replacement prize!'

My tail drooped. Now there was no chance whatsoever that Humphrey Huge Dog was going to get us a spot on the *Hollywoof Canine Spectacular*. I was destined to be a small-town disaster.

But then there was a noise from the back of the crowd...

'Excuse me, excuse me,' said the voice, as dogs moved aside to let Humphrey Huge Dog through.

'Humphrey! This isn't how our performance was supposed to go!' I said.

'What are you talking about?' said Humphrey. 'You boys were hilarious! Fantastic! Pure entertainment!'

I couldn't believe my furry ears!

'This event is always a massive bore, but you two really livened things up! The look on the mayoress' face when you told everyone what she was REALLY thinking! And digging a special hole for the sausages to fall down! Genius! You're natural performers!' continued Humphrey. 'If you want it, there's a place for you on *The Canine Spectacular*! I've got something in mind that will be perfect for you. I'll book you on a flight to Hollywoof tomorrow. The sky's the limit, boys!'

My tail wagged faster than it's ever wagged. I couldn't believe it! We'd snatched victory from the jaws of defeat! I should never have doubted myself! My dream to be the world's most famous sausage dog was still alive.

We were going to Hollywoof!

Chapter 10
FLYING POOCH AIRLINES

Stanley Big Dog and I were running full speed through the airport. Stanley had insisted that we stop off at the Pork Chop Café for travel snacks and now we were seriously late. The airport was a hustle and bustle of holidaymakers and business dogs ready to jet off somewhere much more exciting than Snuffles-by-Sea. But nobody was in more of a rush than us!

'Coming through!' I barked at a group of student Afghan Hounds wearing backpacks. 'Excuse us!'

'Can't we just get the next flight?' panted Stanley, who was carrying both our bags.

'No! We cannot!' I panted back. 'We have to get on this flight or we won't be in Hollywoof in time for the rehearsal.' I took a deep breath. 'And if we miss that, then we might as well just be going on a holiday!'

'Sounds great!' replied Stanley.

'There will be plenty of time for holidays when we're rich and famous,' I said, as we reached the boarding gate with minutes to spare.

Stanley and I boarded the plane: Flight 125 to Hollywoof and our ticket to global stardom! We were heading to *The Canine Spectacular* show, and I couldn't wait. Finally, I was getting my big break – a starring role in the biggest dog performance show in the world.

We stepped on the plane and were greeted by a curly-haired, waggy-tailed cockapoo air steward called Julie. She checked our tickets.

'Welcome on-board, Mr Michael and Mr Stanley! You'll find your baskets in economy class.' Julie pointed to the right, her tail still wagging. 'And you have complimentary chicken chews waiting for you. I hope you have a pleasant flight!'

We weren't famous enough to be sitting in first class yet, but I didn't mind too much because once I was a global superstar, I'd have my own plane.

Stanley bounded down the aisle to find our seats in economy. He'd never flown before and was ridiculously excited. Neither had I, but flying felt like the kind of thing that an almost globally famous sausage dog would take in his furry stride. I sauntered past Julie the air steward, excited to be on my way to Hollywoof. But as I walked past her, my paws started to tingle. Normally I have to tune into a dog's thoughts, but Julie's mind-voice was so strong I could hear it without even trying.

This is SO exciting! My favourite celebrity and they're on my flight! I can't believe it!

I won't lie, I was quite surprised to have bumped into a fan so early on our trip. I mean I was well known in Snuffles-by-Sea, but I wasn't world famous ... yet. But nonetheless, here I was, meeting a massive Michael fan!

'Would you like me to sign a pawtagraph for you?' I asked, giving a little wink.

'Sorry, sir?' replied Julie.

She was clearly a bit nervous about meeting her idol.

'It's always a pleasure to meet a loyal fan,' I said. This was actually the first time, but I was already getting quite used to it.

But strangely, Julie just looked confused rather than star struck. Ah! She must have been told that I wouldn't want a fuss! She was just being professional! I thanked her and trotted down the aisle to find my basket in economy.

I was keen to take Stanley through my

extensive plans for our new show, but he wasn't in his basket. He'd already wandered off – after eating his complimentary chicken chew, and mine as well of course. Knowing Stanley, he was probably trying to get extra snacks from one of the cockapoo air stewards. I settled into my seat. It wasn't as luxurious as the plush-velvet king-sized dog baskets in first class, but it was definitely comfy enough for a nap. I was just closing my eyes when a message came over the loud speaker.

'Ladies and gentledogs, we are experiencing a slight delay due to a missing … item,' said one of the cockapoo air stewards. 'The pilot's squeaky chicken toy isn't where she left it and she's refusing to take off until Sir Squeakalot is found. Could you please all check your seating areas.'

What? A delay to the flight? This was unacceptable.

The loudspeaker message continued. 'Please be aware that we take toy-napping very seriously. If you've seen anything suspicious, please report it to your nearest cockapoo air steward.'

I spotted Julie and called her over immediately.

'Excuse me!' I said. 'We have important business in Hollywoof and can't be late. We're performing at *The Canine Spectacular* and we have a very important rehearsal in a matter of hours!'

'I'm very sorry, sir,' said Julie. 'But this plane isn't going anywhere until Sir Squeakalot is found. The pilot thinks he might have been stolen! Hopefully it won't take long. Our famous passenger in first class is leading the search!'

'Famous passenger?' I said in disbelief. I thought I was the famous passenger! Who could it be?

'Yes! She has such an excellent nose, perfect for searching out a toy!' replied Julie.

An excellent nose? I had a horrible feeling I knew exactly who it was.

I rushed down the aisle and peered through the curtain separating first and economy class. And there she was ... Susan the Chocolate Labrador using her annoying, famous big nose to search under chairs for the missing squeaky toy!

'Michael!' said Susan. 'I didn't know we were on the same flight! So lovely to see you!'

'Oh hello! What a fantastic surprise!' I replied, trying to look pleased to see her. 'Why are you going to Hollywoof? I thought you'd be performing at the Snuffles Corgi Choir

Championship this weekend?'

'Didn't Humphrey tell you?' said Susan. 'We're going to be working together. It's going to be fabulous!'

This was news to me. Humphrey Huge Dog had most definitely NOT shared this important and extremely bothersome piece of information. In fact, I'd tried to call Humphrey on the way to the airport and only got his voicemail telling me he was on holiday!

'But first I need to find Sir Squeakalot or we're not going anywhere!' Susan continued. 'Leave this to me, Michael – I've got it covered!'

And then she winked at me!

I snorted. Susan was trying to steal the limelight from me and we weren't even in Hollywoof yet! If any dog was going to find Sir Squeakalot it was going to be me! I rushed back to my seat. I needed to get Stanley so we could search for the squeaky toy together. He was much better at sniffing than me. Stanley Big Dog wasn't the best of sidekicks, but when sniffing or eating were involved, I could always count on him.

Chapter 11
SIR SQUEAKALOT GETS SQUEAKED –
A LOT

If the flight didn't leave on time, we would be late for *The Canine Spectacular* rehearsals and I wasn't about to let that happen. Stanley Big Dog and I had to find the squeaky toy and return it to the pilot so we could get this plane flying! The only problem was, I couldn't find Stanley…

'I think he's in the loo,' said the French Bulldog in the row behind.

I knocked on the toilet door with my adorable paws. 'Stanley! Are you in there?'

Nothing.

'Stanley! There's a bit of a situation out here! The pilot's squeaky toy has gone missing and we need to find it or we won't get to Hollywoof in time for our rehearsal!'

There was still no reply. What was Stanley up to? I would have to read his mind. It was difficult at first, I'd never read a dog's mind through a door before. But after a bit of concentration, I could hear Stanley's mind-voice.

La la la. Stanley Big Dog singing a song. Dooby, dooby, doo. So Michael can't read his mind. La la la.

'I know you're in there, Stanley!' I replied.

Doo, doo, doo. This is Stanley Big Dog singing a song on the loo!

'Can you come out and help, please, Stanley?'
I said. 'What's taking so long in there?'

Then I remembered the chicken chews,
and Stanley's breakfast of pork chops and his
second breakfast of two T-bone steaks and a
toad in the hole.

'Oh, I see. Well, do what you need to do and
then get out here,' I said.

There was a whippet waiting to use the toilet.
I shook my head. 'If I were you, I'd use the other
toilet.' The whippet nodded in agreement and
trotted off.

But then I heard a strange noise from the
toilet.

SQUEEEAK.

What was that? A mouse? If it was, I'd be
making a complaint to Pooch Airlines!

'Stanley, are you OK?' I asked. 'Is there a
mouse in there?'

SQUEAK. SQUEEEAK.

'Just finish up in there and we can report that pesky mouse to an air steward later. Right now, we need to find Sir Squeakalot! Sir Squeakalot is our priority.'

But then it dawned on me. The terrible truth!

'Stanley, have you got Sir Squeakalot in there?' I asked.

'No,' said Stanley. Sounding a lot like someone who did have Sir Squeakalot in there with him.

'Stanley, is there a chance that you maybe have Sir Squeakalot in there?' I asked gently.

'Maybe,' said Stanley, very quietly.

'I can't believe it! You do realise we could get thrown off the plane for this? We could even be arrested!' I whispered, trying not to draw attention to the fact that my assistant had toy-napped Sir Squeakalot and was seriously jeopardising our chance of global stardom!

SQUEAK. SQUEEEAK.

'Stanley! Can you stop squeaking that thing for one second!' I said. 'We need to work out what to do!'

The toilet cubicle door opened slowly and Stanley Big Dog emerged.

'Sorry, Michael, I didn't know it belonged to anyone,' said Stanley. 'I found it by the drinks trolley and just had to squeak it.'

'Shh! Keep your voice down, Stanley,' I said. 'We'll have to pretend we just found it here.'

And then, just at the time you really don't need a really annoying chocolate Labrador to appear, Susan appeared.

'There's no sign of Sir Squeakalot in first class,' she said. 'Where could he possibly be? The pilot is such a lovely dog. I met her in the first-class lounge! She deserves to be reunited with her squeaky toy!'

I composed myself. 'Actually we've just found Sir Squeakalot in the toilet! Here's the squeaky fellow!'

'How strange! I wonder how he ended up in there!' said Susan, looking suspicious.

'Very strange!' I said.

'It hasn't been squeaked!' blurted out Stanley. 'It's very unsqueaked!'

'Good! I should hope not!' said Susan.

'And it definitely hasn't been squeaked by a big dog!' added Stanley Big Dog.

I glared at Stanley.

Susan cocked her head to one side and looked at Sir Squeakalot, then she gave him a good sniff. There was a large glob of Stanley slobber dripping down one side. I held my breath.

'Fabulous,' said Susan. 'Well, we've all

done a great job at finding him, so well done everybody!'

I was just about to pick up Sir Squeakalot and take it to the pilot when Susan's nosey schnoz swooped in. 'Probably best if I return it, Michael! Since I've already met the pilot.'

Susan paused. And looked me straight in the eye.

'And we don't want the pilot thinking that you or Stanley had anything to do with Sir Squeakalot going missing...' she added.

We were rumbled. And Susan left me no choice – if we didn't let her return Sir Squeakalot she'd drop me and Stanley right in the doo-doo. So the glory would have to be Susan's. As usual.

One day I would be sitting in first class. One day I would be more famous than Susan the Chocolate Labrador. And maybe one day,

Stanley Big Dog would behave himself. But for now, I had to be patient. Once I had proved myself at *The Canine Spectacular*, it would be my time to shine.

There was a round of apawse from the rest of the plane as Susan walked down the aisle. I turned to see her transporting Sir Squeakalot back to the pilot ... on her nose! Such a show-off!

Just as Susan was about to disappear behind the first-class curtain, she turned to look at me. 'Well done on finding Sir Squeakalot, Michael.

I'm really looking forward to working with you.'

'Thanks, Susan!' I replied. Maybe she wasn't so bad after all!

But then she added, 'I've never had an assistant before!'

I couldn't believe what I was hearing. Susan's assistant! Her assistant! Susan's! This was outrageous. I needed to speak to Humphrey Huge Dog as soon as we touched down in Hollywoof. I was not born to be an assistant – I was born to be a superstar!

Chapter 12
WHERE'S MY CONFETTI CANNON?

Stanley Big Dog and I touched down at Hollywoof airport and bounded straight to the taxi rank.

'Hollywoof Theatre! On Hollywoof Main Street! As fast as you can!' I barked at the taxi driver.

I'd tried to get Humphrey Huge Dog on the phone to clear up this whole business about me being Susan's assistant, but he was on holiday in the south of France. Probably getting pawdicures, eating gourmet doggie dinners and lounging by the swimming pool! Typical! So, Stanley and I were now on our way to the theatre to talk to the stage manager instead. Urgently!

Stanley didn't seem at all concerned with our predicament – he was too busy enjoying himself, with his head stuck out the window and his ears flapping in the wind.

Hollywoof Main Street was lined with palm trees and stylish dogs wearing sunglasses. I spotted a Great Dane on roller skates and there were gold-plated wee stations at the foot of every palm tree! But of course, I couldn't really enjoy taking in the sights with so much on my mind. There was no way I was playing second fiddle to Susan. Me – a sidekick? I should be the star of the show! And anyway, if I was the sidekick, where would that leave Stanley Big Dog? Sidekicks don't have sidekicks! This was getting ridiculous!

We arrived at Hollywoof Theatre: an enormous building that was probably ten times as big as the Grand Fancy Theatre Royale back in Snuffles-by-Sea. And with a domed roof and twirly pillars either side of the huge entrance, it actually looked like a palace!

I rushed inside, with an over-excited Stanley Big Dog close behind. Framed pictures of famous dogs lined the walls including Elvis Pawsley and the world's favourite magician, the Great Houndini. Arriving at the Hollywoof Theatre should have been the greatest moment of my life so far, but instead I was too busy trying to save my career before it had even begun.

'I need to speak to the stage manager, immediately,' I said to the French Bulldogs on ticket sales in the entrance hall. 'This cannot wait!'

One of the French Bulldogs cocked his head to one side and looked us both up and down. 'Oh, you must be Susan's sidekicks here for the rehearsal. Bernadette's expecting you; she's in her office. Straight past the VIP dressing rooms, third door on the right.'

If one more dog called me Susan's sidekick, I might explode.

Stanley and I headed backstage to sort out this complete and utter mess-up. We found Bernadette in her office. She was a huge St Bernard and was pacing around like the weight of the world was on her furry shoulders.

'Come in, come in – but I haven't got long!' she said. 'There's a problem with the programmes and the steak and kidney ice creams for the interval haven't arrived! I'm not paid enough for this!'

'I'm Michael the Mind-Reading Sausage Dog,' I replied. 'I'm afraid we have a major problem! And it's much, much worse than a lack of doggy ice creams.'

'Oh, you must be Susan's assistants,' said Bernadette. 'If you're here to complain about the shared dressing room for the minor talent, there's nothing that can be done. I know the dancing corgis can be a pain, but they really have to practise that salsa dancing as much as possible.'

'No, it's not that,' I replied. 'I think there's been a mistake. I'm not supposed to be an assistant. I have my own talent! Humphrey has arranged for us to have our own slot on the show.'

'I think there may have been a misunderstanding,' replied Bernadette. 'I have you both on the list as assistants. And what's on the list is final!'

'The thing is, Bernadette … I'm a really big deal in Snuffles-by-Sea and I think it would be much more appropriate for Stanley and me have to have our own slot on the show.'

'That's just not possible,' said Bernadette. 'We don't want any last-minute changes to affect Susan's performance. We're so lucky to have her this season – the audience are going to love her!'

I swallowed my growing frustration like a gristly bit of pork chop. 'Perhaps we could just have a small slot to start with? After Susan's performance?' I suggested. 'And we can make it a bigger slot when you see how much the audience loves us. Which of course, they will!'

'Well, that would be a problem, you see, because there won't be enough time to move Susan's confetti cannon,' replied Bernadette.

'Susan's got a … confetti cannon?' I asked. I'd always dreamed of having my own confetti cannon.

'Yes, it will really compliment the indoor fireworks we're going to let off when she balances each peanut,' said Bernadette. 'Quite the spectacle! The audience is going to love it!'

I took a deep breath. I knew what the audience would love, and it was me: Michael the Amazing Mind-Reading Sausage Dog, assisted by Stanley Big Dog!

Bernadette had now launched into a long list of sidekick tasks that Stanley and I would be responsible for.

'Michael, you'll be introducing Susan,' said Bernadette. 'We might get you to do a bit of mind-reading, but not necessarily. You'll also have the important task of peanut transportation.'

My blood was boiling, as I smiled and nodded.

Bernadette continued. 'The main thing is that you make sure Susan's peanuts are always close at hand for her fantastic act.'

'And what about Stanley? What will he be doing?' I asked.

'Stanley will have the very important task of firing the confetti cannon at the end of Susan's amazing performance!'

'Exciting!' said Stanley, sniffing at the confetti sacks.

I took a deep breath. If I couldn't persuade Bernadette now, I would just have to impress her as Susan's assistant. I could still be a *Canine Spectacular Hollywoof* superstar; it would just take a little longer than I'd originally planned.

'Jeepers! Look at the time!' said Bernadette. 'Rehearsals start soon! You boys can drop your bags in the dressing room for minor talent, sidekicks and backing singers.'

Stanley and I made our way down the corridor. Stanley was annoyingly still buzzing about his new job as the firer of Susan's confetti cannon. I was still getting used to the idea of a shared dressing room. Maybe it wouldn't be as bad as I thought. But then we opened the door and I realised that it was.

The shared dressing room was packed with more dogs than the population of Snuffles-By-Sea! There were greyhounds practising their singing scales, cocker spaniels trying on tutus and an entire dance troupe of corgis running through a salsa routine in the middle of everything. I took a deep breath … and swallowed a cloud of hairspray created by a golden retriever trying to style her hair into a quiff. I deserved my own dressing room, with my name on the door and a constant supply of tasty treats. But that would have to wait – for now I just had to find enough space in this dressing room so that I wouldn't be pressed up against Stanley's armpit. Or worse.

'There's some space over here if you need it!' barked a small greyhound with a big voice. 'Room for a small one … and a big one!' he said, looking at Stanley and pointing to a pokey corner next to a group of singing greyhounds.

Stanley and I made our way through the chaotic tangle of dogs, including salsa dancing our way through the corgi performers.

'Thanks!' I said, as we finally reached the one remaining space in the whole dressing room.

'My name's Arnold. I'm part of Greyhounds of Sound,' said the dog who'd called us over. 'We're an acapella choir.'

'Nice to meet you,' I said, shaking his paw. Stanley and I crammed ourselves into the corner.

'What do you boys do?' asked Arnold.

'Well, we're helping out with Susan's act,' I replied.

'Fantastic! We're Susan's backing singers, so we'll be working together!' said Arnold.

'Susan's got backing singers AND two sidekicks?' I asked in disbelief.

'Yeah, she's top of the bill this season!' said Arnold. 'We're just here to make her look good!'

'Actually, Stanley and I are only doing this temporarily. I'm a professional mind-reader and I'm hoping to get my own slot soon.'

'You and every other dog in here! Good luck, mate, but it's a tough business to crack!' said Arnold. 'Wait, didn't you have bags with you?'

I glanced around. Where were our bags?!

'Stanley! What have you done with the bags?' I said.

'I had them just a minute ago,' replied Stanley.

'I can't believe we've lost the bags! I thought you had the bags!' I barked. This was the worst day ever.

'I don't know where they are, Michael. I'm sure I had them with me, then I sat down and they were gone,' said Stanley.

I was just about to rush around turning the dressing room upside down when I noticed a luggage tag poking out from underneath Stanley's bum.

'You're sitting on them, Stanley!' I barked.

'Am I?' asked Stanley, standing up to reveal our two completely squished bags. 'Oh yes, there they are!'

I sighed. This was not how I'd imagined my Hollywoof debut – as an assistant to Susan with a bag full of crumpled glittery waistcoats that I no longer needed.

But there was no time to wallow. Bernadette appeared at the dressing-room door. 'Can we have Greyhounds of Sound, and Susan's sidekicks to the stage, please?'

We hurried after Bernadette and found Susan already in the spotlight. She was standing on a podium wearing a purple feather boa and balancing a peanut on her nose like it was a gold nugget. Standard Susan.

'Oh, hello! Didn't see you there,' said Susan, leaping off her podium. 'Hi Michael! Hi Bradley Big Dog!'

'It's actually Stanley Big Dog,' I replied. Not that Stanley cared, he'd wandered off to look at the confetti cannon.

'That's what I said!' said a smiling Susan. 'So great to be working with you both. My last assistant, Daisy, was great – but it turned out she had a peanut allergy!'

'That's such a shame,' I said, trying to hold in my jealousy of Daisy's lucky escape. 'Bernadette mentioned that I would get the opportunity to use my mind-reading skills!'

'Of course!' said Susan. 'It would be crazy not to showcase your amazing talent! We want you to read the minds of audience members...'

My ears pricked up. Maybe things were looking up!

'...And tell me whether they want me to balance a peanut, a cashew nut, a hazelnut or a coconut,' added Susan. 'Or sometimes how many nuts in total!'

OK, this sounded very nut-focused, but maybe I could work with this.

'While wearing the costume, of course,' added Susan.

'There's a costume?' I asked nervously.

'Can somebody fetch the costume for Michael?' barked Bernadette.

'What costume?' I said. I rarely trusted another dog's taste. Unless it had sequins, it was likely to be ghastly. 'Can't Stanley wear the costume?'

'Stanley couldn't possibly fit in the peanut suit,' said Bernadette.

My face dropped as one of the springer spaniels from the crew appeared carrying a costume shaped like a peanut in its shell.

'Try it on!' said Susan. 'It's just your size!'

I reluctantly stepped into the suit, which Susan seemed to take a little too much glee in zipping up.

'Is this really necessary?' I asked, pushing my snout out of the peanut hood.

'I love it!' said Stanley Big Dog unhelpfully.

'The suit comes with the job,' said Bernadette impatiently. 'If you don't want to be Susan's assistant then tell me now, because I'll need to find someone else. And there are plenty of other dogs who would jump at the chance!'

'No, no, it's fine,' I replied. 'I'm sure I'll get used to it.'

The peanut suit was already making me itch. But I would have to go along with this madness for a while. Nobody likes a diva. Especially a diva in a peanut suit.

Chapter 13
MICHAEL THE ASSISTANT
MIND-READING PEANUT

I was not living the Hollywoof dream. Stanley and I were sharing a house with the Greyhounds of Sound just outside of the city, and while they were nice-enough chaps, they were extremely messy housemates. Even messier than Stanley! And getting a good night's sleep was impossible thanks to the greyhounds' late-night singing practice in the early hours of the morning.

I belonged in the Hollywoof Hills with the big stars! Susan, Tremelo (the opera-singing

Great Dane) and the other headliners at *The Canine Spectacular* were staying in spectacular mansions with velvet king-size dog baskets and huge water fountains. They even had red carpets leading out to specially planted trees for weeing on! AND … they had stretch limos to take them to the theatre every night. We had to travel on the local bus! I tried not to think about Susan with her paws up in her very own limo. I had to be patient. My time would come.

At the theatre, Stanley and I would squeeze ourselves into the shared dressing room for minor talent. I would reluctantly change out of my fabulous waistcoat into the peanut suit. Susan would take to the stage and, when she gave me the signal, I would trot on wearing the peanut suit and carrying peanuts in the pockets. The only part of the show where I got to demonstrate any talent was at the very end when an audience member was selected to choose how many peanuts they wanted Susan to balance while blindfolded. It was my job to mind-read the number of peanuts they wanted. I'd never liked peanuts. And now I hated them. But if I wanted to have my own slot on the show, I just had to stick with this and work my way up.

But real talent cannot be contained – one way or another it will find a way to show itself. And one night, I found a way to shine just a little bit more…

Like every other night, I trotted onto the stage in peanut mode for the final bit of Susan's act. Susan had already selected a poodle volunteer, and Percy the Poodle was poised and ready for me to read his mind.

'Welcome to Susan's Amazing Peanut Balancing Show,' I said, doing the required peanut twirl. 'I'm Michael, the Assistant Mind-Reading Peanut!'

The audience loved this bit. I suppose I did look adorable. But I didn't want to look adorable! I was a professional, not a peanut!

'Percy, please stand still and think of a number,' I said. 'Don't say it out loud.'

Percy stood very still and stared into the distance.

'The number you're thinking will be the number of peanuts Susan will balance on her nose … while blindfolded!' I added.

I could hear the swishing of tails wagging in the audience. Despite the fact they'd already watched Susan balance peanuts in various different poses for the last ten minutes, they still wanted to watch her balance more peanuts! These dogs were easily pleased. If I had the chance to entertain them without Susan cramping my style, it would blow their minds!

I got my head back in the game and focused on reading Percy's mind. As usual, my paws began to tingle and my ears began to twitch. Frankly, reading the minds of dogs was a walkies in the park. I could do it in my sleep!

'The number of peanuts you're thinking of is … SEVEN PEANUTS!' I announced.

'That's right!' barked Percy. And the audience went wild.

Susan took a little bow even though it was me that had read Percy's mind! She started putting her blindfold on.

And that's when I did it.

I took a deep breath and did the unthinkable.

I went off script.

'You're also thinking about having a roast chicken ice cream in the interval,' I blurted out. 'And you really like peanuts because they remind you of when you were a small poodle pup and your mum used to balance them on her nose to cheer you up if you'd had a bad day at puppy school.'

The audience fell silent. Susan whipped off her blindfold and stared at me.

Percy's mouth dropped open. 'That's amazing! Can I get your pawtograph? Or maybe a selfie with you for my Instagrowl?'

Tails were swishing in the audience. And they were swishing for me!

'Thank you to my Assistant Mind-Reading Peanut!' barked Susan quickly, grabbing seven peanuts from the pocket of my peanut suit and shoving me off the stage.

After that, much to Susan's horror, Bernadette extended my mind-reading part by a whole two minutes! I was making progress and beginning to build a small fanbase as Michael the Assistant Mind-Reading Peanut. My fans called themselves The Chipolatas and chanted my name when Susan called me onto stage. They were usually drowned out by the sound of Susan's fans, and they often had seats right at the back, but I had fans!

But, of course, I didn't want to be famous for being an assistant mind-reading peanut, I wanted to be famous in my own right. I was Michael the Amazing Mind-Reading Sausage Dog and I was ready to be the star of my own slot on *The Canine Spectacular*. How long would I have to wait?

Chapter 14
THE DOG POOP HITS THE FAN

A few weeks later, on a night like any other, I trotted backstage to check that Stanley Big Dog had picked up his performance waistcoat from the dry cleaners (there had been an incident with a plate of particularly sticky barbecue ribs). But before I could find him, I was greeted by a very strange sight. All of the other dogs were in complete silence, even Susan, who was usually boring someone to death about the perfect peanut shape. Bernadette, the St Bernard stage manager, was rushing around like she was desperate for a wee.

'What are we going to do? This is a disaster!' she barked.

No dog said anything.

'What's happened?' I asked.

'Everyone's got kennel cough! Everyone!' said Bernadette. 'We'll have to cancel the show! We can't put on a show if no dog can talk!'

My heart was beating faster. I was born for moments like these.

'Not everyone,' I said. 'I'm fine! I'll just have to open the show. And close the show. And do the bit in the middle of the show.'

'Really?' said Bernadette, perking up.

'Of course!' I replied, over the moon at the opportunity to put on a fabulous one dog show.

Tremelo, the opera-singing Great Dane, coughed and spluttered. And I realised that I was perhaps looking a bit too excited about the fact that everyone was ill.

'Of course, it's only until you're all feeling

better. I do hope you all get well...' But at the end of my good wishes, my words disappeared! I tried to speak but all that came out was a raspy cough. I couldn't believe it – I was ill too!

Bernadette's mouth dropped open. 'Oh fiddlesticks! Now we really are in trouble!'

And we were.

Bernadette went back into panic mode. 'The show's tonight and we've already sold all the tickets! There's no dog left who can perform!'

But then I heard a familiar voice...

I had spent so much time with Stanley that I could hear his mind-voice even when he wasn't close by. It was coming from the costume cupboard...

These sausages are Stanley's sausages! Good job everyone's got that weird illness and nobody's making me share them. Stanley Big Dog never gets ill!

This was great news! Stanley didn't have kennel cough. At this stage I didn't really know how this helped the situation, but Stanley was our only hope and we had to do something. If the show bombed, I'd never get my own slot on *The Canine Spectacular*!

I got Bernadette's attention with a combination of paw sign language and hoarse barks, and led her to Stanley. We found him in the costume cupboard gobbling sausages among the feather boas and glittery waistcoats.

'But what can Stanley do on his own?' she asked, looking unconvinced that Stanley Big Dog could save the day.

Stanley wolfed down another sausage.

I shrugged my furry shoulders. I wasn't sure, but Stanley had to be talented at something...

Chapter 15
STANLEY'S SPECIAL TALENT

It turned out that Stanley did have a talent. We weren't sure how it would go down with the audience, but it was our only hope. I sat in the wings curled under a blanket, hoping that just the presence of me and my outstanding talent would rub off on Stanley.

The curtain went up and Stanley Big Dog addressed a confused-looking audience.

'Hello, I'm Stanley and this evening I'm going to … eat sausages really fast!'

The audience fell silent.

There was a banner saying 'Stanley Big Dog's Sausage Spectacular', and two of the French Bulldogs from ticket sales had been persuaded to dance around behind Stanley wearing feather boas. The audience didn't look impressed.

Bernadette rushed on with a string of sausages so long that nobody was quite sure where the end was. But it soon became clear that we had underestimated just how quickly Stanley Big Dog can eat sausages.

Within seconds Stanley had eaten every single sausage.

'It's OK!' barked Bernadette. 'We've got an emergency sausage supply backstage! We'll just have to think on our paws and get Stanley to do some tricks that will make them last a bit longer.'

Stanley sat in the middle of the stage waiting for the extra sausages. I could see the audience waiting to be entertained. I wished I could go and wow them with my act, but my voice was still croaky and I felt so ill I couldn't move from beneath my blanket.

The extra sausages were rushed onto the stage and Stanley continued his act, with highlights including:

- Stanley jumps for sausages
- Stanley chases his tail while eating sausages
- Stanley sits at the back of the stage eating sausages and scratching himself

It will come as no surprise to you that the Stanley Big Dog Sausage Spectacular didn't go down very well. Theatre critic Barbara Barkington-Truffle gave it a terrible review and described it as:

A catastrophe of epic proportions that even sausage lovers will hate! Don't go to this show unless you're intending to have a very long nap.

Barbara Barkington-Truffle,
Paws & Hound

Barbara Barkington-Truffle is well respected in the entertainment industry and even when we all recovered from kennel cough, ticket sales took a massive hit.

This was terrible. Any other dog would have given up at this point. But not me. Anyone can have a dream while they're napping in a warm basket with a belly full of roast chicken. It takes a real star to keep following that dream when things go wrong. I knew that I could save the show. I just needed my chance to shine.

Chapter 16
GO BIG OR GO HOME

After the terrible reviews of Stanley's show, things went downhill fast. *The Canine Spectacular* had become unpopular overnight. Hollywoof might as well have cocked its leg up and had a long wee on the show. On one night the only dogs in the audience were two Boston Terriers and a golden retriever who'd won a free ticket in a competition at his local grooming salon. And, just when we thought things couldn't get any worse, a major problem sprang up right across the road...

Bernadette called a meeting backstage.

'We've got a serious problem,' said Bernadette. 'Wolfgang and Schnitzel are in town. And their new show is set to break box office records – tonight's opening show is already sold out!'

'We can't compete with superstar magicians!' said Tremelo the Opera Singing Great Dane. 'My nieces love Wolfgang and Schnitzel – everyone loves them!'

'Well, I've never heard of them,' said one of the Greyhounds of Sound. 'Why should we be worried about some boring magicians?'

I hadn't heard of them either, but from the look on Bernadette's face it was obvious we should be extremely worried. She pulled a magazine out of her bag. On the front cover there was a giant schnauzer fanning some playing cards and a sandy-coloured Chihuahua about to saw an Afghan Hound in half.

Bernadette opened the magazine and read aloud: 'Global sensations, magicians Wolfgang and Schnitzel are set to take Hollywoof by storm with their new show, Wolfgang and Schnitzel's *Magic by Moonlight*. A show that will blow your mind – if you only see one show in Hollywoof, see this one. And if you see two, see this one twice!'

'This is a disaster!' said Susan. 'Who's going to come to our show if everyone's over there!'

'We're going to be the only show in Hollywoof with no audience!' said Tremelo.

'I'm afraid it's worse than that,' said Bernadette, looking even more stressed than usual. 'If we can't compete with *Magic by Moonlight*, then *The Canine Spectacular* will be cancelled … PERMANENTLY.'

This was my worst nightmare. If the show was cancelled, I would never get my chance to escape the peanut suit and get my own slot on *The Canine Spectacular*!

'I've spoken to Humphrey Huge Dog and he's asked us to come up with ideas to reinvent the show,' said Bernadette. 'He'll be joining us once he's finished some important business in the south of France.'

'Never fear! I'm here!' barked a loud voice in the corridor.

We all turned to see Humphrey Huge Dog burst through the door.

'Hello everyone! Got an early flight when I heard the poop had hit the fan over here! Fantastic to see you all! So how are we going to give this show a boot up the backside?' asked Humphrey. 'What ideas have you got so far?'

I stepped forward but Tremelo, the Opera Singing Great Dane, beat me to it.

'Maybe we could get some new posters,' suggested Tremelo. 'Or give out free roast chicken ice creams to the first one hundred dogs?'

'No, it needs to be something spectacular!' said Humphrey. 'Something that will truly wow the audience!'

'Well, balancing a peanut on your nose is already spectacular,' said Susan. 'I'm not sure it's possible to make it more exciting.'

For the first time ever, Susan and I were in complete agreement.

'Humphrey's right,' I said. 'We need to think big! Really big!'

'But not too expensive,' said Bernadette. 'Unfortunately, we've blown most of the budget on Susan's deluxe feather boas.'

'I don't mind eating some more sausages,' said Stanley, trying to be helpful.

'That's what got us into this mess in the first place,' said Susan.

'Stanley tried his best,' I replied. 'And maybe if he'd had a bit more time to prepare, speed sausage-eating could have been the next big thing!'

Susan didn't look convinced.

'What about me?' I suggested. 'If I had my own slot and my own confetti cannon, I think I could be really spectacular!'

'No offence, Michael, but you've got a very small nose,' said Susan. 'Best leave the peanut balancing to the experts.'

'Not peanut balancing – I'd do my mind-reading act!' I replied. 'I think I've proved myself over the last few weeks. Being Susan's assistant has been a good experience, but I wasn't born to be a peanut, I was born to be a star.'

Humphrey's ears pricked up and he stared at me with his head cocked to one side.

We all waited to hear what Humphrey thought.

'I love it!' barked Humphrey.

Stanley's tail was wagging out of control. I was too nervous to wag mine. Was this my moment?

'Susan will be the star and you'll be the less-talented, but enthusiastic challenger!' said Humphrey. 'We'll pit you against Susan in a challenge event. I can see the posters now – Spectacular Susan vs The Underdog!'

Underdog! My name wasn't even going to be on the poster! My heart sank, but I didn't let my frustration show.

'Let's do it!' I barked. It was time for my inner superstar to finally shine. This new show had to work. And if it didn't, we'd all be out of a job. And Stanley and I would be on the first flight back to Snuffles-by-Sea.

Chapter 17
THIS IS NUTS!

On the big day, the theatre was packed. News had travelled fast and dogs from across Hollywoof and the world were eagerly awaiting the *Susan vs The Underdog Challenge Showdown Extravaganza*. Word on the street was that Wolfgang and Schnitzel were no longer the only hot ticket in town. And now we just needed to prove that our new show lived up to the hype. Unfortunately for the audience, they'd have to watch boring Susan first. But then it would be time for my showstopping solo Hollywoof debut, with Stanley Big Dog, of course.

I peeked through the red-velvet stage curtain and spotted Barbara Barkington-Truffle – the reviewer was back! If we could impress Barbara, then the future of *The Canine Spectacular* would be safe. Sitting next to her was Frankie Floofle Toes! THE Frankie Floofle Toes! Frankie 'TV Producer Extraordinaire' Floofle Toes! Rumour had it that Frankie was on the hunt for a star to front a brand-new TV show. I just had to give the best performance of my life and outshine Susan, then that TV show would be mine!

'Positions, please! Curtain in one minute!' barked Bernadette.

The backstage crew wheeled on a huge countdown clock – it would be used to time me and Susan doing our challenges. Whoever finished in the quickest time was the winner.

Stanley and I waited in the wings for our big moment. This was the moment I had been waiting for my whole life. I was also waiting for the moment I got to design my own range of Michael waistcoats, but I would just have to wait a little bit longer for that.

The audience woofed and howled with excitement as Susan took to the stage. 'Welcome Ladies and Gentledogs,' she barked, 'to the very first Challenge Extravaganza! Tonight, I'll be balancing peanuts on my nose … while completing an extremely difficult obstacle course! Against the clock!'

Susan gave a little bow and soaked up the apawse.

'And good luck to my challenger tonight,' she continued. 'The absolutely fantastic miniature sausage dog, Michael! Small, but very talented! Michael will be attempting his challenge later when he'll be trying to read the minds of every dog breed from A to Z! Also against the clock! And hopefully he'll be wearing that peanut suit that you all know and love!'

I took a deep breath. I most definitely would not be wearing that peanut suit. And hopefully after tonight, I would never have to wear it again.

Susan had quickly moved on to talking about herself and was pumping up the audience with a boring anecdote about how she first got into peanut balancing.

'People often ask me for tips on how to get into peanut balancing,' Susan bored on. 'Well, at age two, I came to peanut balancing much later in life than many dogs. The thing about peanuts is that they're very knobbly so you need a very flat snout to stop them rolling off.'

So boring! So ridiculously boring in fact that I nodded off! I was dreaming about freshly laundered waistcoats and a sell-out show, when...

'Peanuts!' barked one of the backstage dogs. 'Where are the peanuts!'

My eyes sprang open and I was greeted by a stampede of dogs rushing around.

'How can they be missing?' barked Bernadette.

Susan was on stage looking distraught. She was primed and ready to balance peanuts on her nose, but there were no peanuts. Not one.

I lifted my head up from the bag of peanuts I had been resting on and looked around to see where Stanley Big Dog was.

Wait! Bag of peanuts! I was lying on Susan's peanuts!

I looked around. Nobody had noticed that I'd been napping on Susan's nuts. It was like time stood still. And slowly but surely a thought crossed my mind.

What if I didn't tell anyone that I had been accidentally concealing Susan's nuts? What if Susan failed to complete her challenge because there were no peanuts? And what if I was the dog to wow the audience? I could save the show all by myself and become a global superstar just like I'd always wanted. All I had to do was sit back down and say nothing.

But then I spotted Stanley. He was looking for the peanuts while desperately trying not to get distracted by the roast chicken ice creams that were being wheeled past him.

'Michael!' barked Stanley. 'Can you check for the peanuts under the costume wardrobe, I can't fit under there!'

Stanley was trying to help and just wanted the best for everyone. How could I look him in the face again if I cheated? There was a lump in my throat as I caught myself in one of the backstage mirrors. Staring back at me was a superstar sausage dog in a purple waistcoat and sequinned bow tie. A superstar sausage dog who wanted to wow the audience with his talent, not by taking shortcuts and sitting on another dog's bag of peanuts. I wanted to win this competition fair and square. I took a deep breath, stood tall and dragged the nuts onto the stage.

'Michael's found them!' barked Stanley.

For once, Susan looked pleased to see me. The countdown clock was started and she was finally able to begin her challenge. I quickly rushed off the stage before the audience could notice me.

This was Susan's moment.

Sometimes you have to be the bigger dog, even when you're the smaller dog.

Chapter 18
A FURRY NEMESIS

Susan placed the peanuts on her nose and the countdown clock began. The obstacle course facing her was extremely challenging. There was a balance beam, a wobbly see-saw and a multi-coloured ball pit – and that was just the first section! But as Susan nailed each hurdle and balance beam with ease, I started to get worried. Could I really complete my challenge? What if I wasn't as good as I thought? What if, after everything, Susan was actually more talented than me? I watched and waited.

But as Susan negotiated the final obstacle, a misjudged wink at Frankie Floofle Toes led to a catastrophic stumble. Peanuts were sent flying everywhere and Susan's challenge was over!

Susan came off stage and I tried to offer some words of support. 'Susan, that was really bad luck. Are you OK?'

I was surprised to find that I actually did feel bad for Susan.

'You don't have to feel bad for me, Michael,' replied Susan as she walked past. 'It's not like you're going to complete your challenge anyway.'

And then I didn't feel bad for Susan any more. Instead, I felt a growl in the pit of my stomach. Not the growl that Stanley's stomach makes when he hasn't had a sausage all morning. The growl that grows inside you when somebody thinks you're not good enough. The growl that fires you up and pushes you to prove that you're not the underdog. I was Michael the Amazing Mind-Reading Sausage Dog. And it was time to show the world!

After a short interval for the audience to fill up on roast chicken ice creams, it was finally my moment. I took to the stage and the curtain rose.

'Ladies and gentledogs!' I announced. 'Welcome to the greatest show in Hollywoof … and possibly on Earth!'

All eyes were on me, including the eyes of TV producer, Frankie Floofle Toes and the theatre-show reviewer, Barbara Barkington-Truffle. The rest of the cast were all counting on me.

'Today I will be wowing you by setting a new world record for reading the minds of twenty-six dog breeds, from A to Z,' I continued. 'Each dog has written down their favourite thing on a board, only seen by them. Prepare to be more amazed than you've ever been before!'

A couple of huskies in the front row howled with appreciation.

'Stanley, bring on the dogs!' I barked.

Stanley bounded onto the stage, followed by a procession of various dogs of all shapes, sizes and fur types. They all hopped up on to individual podiums in a line, ready to have their minds read.

'And not only will I be reading the minds of twenty-six dogs – I will be doing it AGAINST THE CLOCK!' I announced.

'Can somebody give me a countdown, please,' I asked, getting myself into position next to the Afghan Hound for letter A.

The audience chanted, '5! 4! 3! 2! 1!'

Stanley started the countdown clock – I had

ten minutes to make my dream come true!

The dogs for A to O were straightforward and I rattled through the first half of the alphabet with ease.

DOG	FAVOURITE THING
• Adonis the Afghan Hound	Chewing a big sock
• Barry the beagle	Walks in the park
• Copper the corgi	Sausages
• Diego the Dalmatian	Sausages
• Evie the English Bulldog	Sausages
• Furball the fox terrier	Pork chops
• Goliath the German Shepherd	Sausages
• Herbie the Havana Silk Dog	Chasing squirrels
• Idris the Irish Wolfhound	Top hats
• Juniper the Jack Russell	Roast chicken ice cream
• Kipper the Kerry Blue Terrier	Sniffing bums

• Luna the Labrador	Digging holes for no reason
• Matilda the minature schnauzer	Jazz singing
• Niles the Norwegian Elkhound	Chewing on a big stick
• Otto the otterhound	Sausages

I was in my element! Everything was going swimmingly. Nothing could stop me! I turned to the next dog ready to nail another mind-reading, but instead of glory, I was snout to snout with … A PUG. My nemesis!

I muttered to Stanley under my breath, 'I told you not to get a pug!'

'Did you?' replied Stanley. 'I thought you said don't get a mug.'

'Why would I say that?' I barked. 'That's not a dog breed!'

'Well, I thought it was a bit weird, but you always know best, Michael,' said Stanley.

'Why didn't you get a poodle!' I asked, panicking. 'Or a Pekingese! Or a Pomeranian! Anything but a pug!'

The small pug started shuffling around. 'Hi, I'm Patrick. I'm your biggest fan, Michael!' he snuffled. 'This is the best moment of my life! I mean, I'm only ten months old but I'm sure it's going to be the best moment of my life and I haven't even lived it yet!'

I gulped. This tiny pug was my WORST NIGHTMARE. I was facing the one dog breed that I had never been able to mind read.

'I'm having my mind read by Michael the Assistant Mind-Reading Peanut,' continued Patrick. 'This is the coolest thing ever!'

I glanced at the clock. Five minutes left. I needed much longer than five minutes! Working out how to read the mind of a pug might take me a lifetime! Longer than a lifetime ... forever!

'Very nice to meet you,' I replied, trying to look like my usual superstar self and not like I was standing on the edge of failure. A small, snuffly fan-pug puppy called Patrick was about to be my downfall.

Chapter 19
AN UNEXPECTED HERO

Patrick the pug gazed at me with adoring eyes. If I failed to read his mind, I would fail my challenge … and break his heart! And I could say goodbye to that TV show. But the worst thing? I would prove Susan right, that I wasn't a superstar and that I belonged in Snuffles-By-Sea. Not Hollywoof.

The audience were getting restless.

Maybe I could just guess what Patrick's favourite thing was? Most of the dogs were thinking about sausages anyway. But what if it was sausages swimming in gravy? Or a very specific type of sausage? I couldn't risk it.

All I could hear was the giant clock counting down and Bernadette pacing back and forth backstage. With every tick of the clock, I felt my dream slipping away.

There was only one thing for it – I would have to try to read Patrick's mind and hope for the best.

I got into my usual mind-reading stance. I focused and desperately hoped that my paws would start to tingle and my ears begin to twitch.

'Should I sit differently?' snuffled Patrick. 'I can stand up on two legs if that helps!'

Patrick energetically tried to stand up on two legs and landed in a heap. But Patrick's mind-voice was nowhere to be heard. Just like with Priscilla the pug in the Snuffles-By-Sea talent show, I was failing. All over again! Reading a pug's mind was an impossible task. Yes, I was ridiculously talented at mind-reading, but when it came to pugs, I was useless!

I looked over to the side of the stage. The Greyhounds of Sound were pacing around with worry, and Bernadette's face was pure panic. I was letting everyone down.

I took a deep breath. The dream was over. There was nothing more I could do.

But then I heard something familiar. The mind-voice of Stanley Big Dog ... and for once it wasn't thinking about pork chops or chasing a squirrel.

Come on, Michael. Stanley Big Dog knows you can do it! You'll work it out!

Stanley's tail was wagging as he looked at me with his tongue hanging out.

Stanley believed in me! And if Stanley believed in me, then maybe I could believe in myself! Maybe I could do this after all. I picked myself up and took another look at Patrick the pug. My paws still weren't tingling and my ears definitely weren't twitching, but my nose could definitely smell something … I leant in closer and had a little sniff. Peanut butter!

And as Patrick jiggled around trying to help me read his mind better, I noticed some crispy brown leaves on his furry legs.

'Three minutes left!' barked Bernadette in the wings.

The crowd were up on their seats and cheering for me. I had to do this!

'I've got it!' I said, taking a deep breath. 'Patrick, your favourite hobby is eating peanut butter while rolling around in autumn leaves!' I announced.

'That's right!' said Patrick with glee. Stanley Big Dog revealed the answer on the board and the crowd went wild.

I gave Stanley a little nod. I was starting to realise that even superstars need a helping paw every now and again. I took a deep breath. I could still do this.

Next in the line-up were:

DOG	FAVOURITE THING
• Quentin the Queensland Heeler	Sausages
• Rolo the rottweiler	Naps
• Snoopy the springer spaniel	Rolling in muddy puddles
• Titan the Tibetan Terrier	Staring at pigeons
• Ulysses the ultimate mastiff	A squeaky toy called Mr Piggy Wig
• Vinnie the viszla	Listening to opera
• Winnie the West Highland Terrier	Massive sausages

And then a dog breed beginning with X that is very difficult to pronounce. You can try if you want. Or if someone else is reading this to you, then they can give it a go, but it's very difficult so I won't hold out much hope that they'll get it right. The dog breed is…

THE XOLOITZCUINTLI

Yep, completely wrong. It's also known as the Mexican Hairless Dog so I'll help you out by calling it that from now on.

After the Mexican Hairless Dog, there was a Yorkshire Terrier and after that there was a zuchon. And after that?

Glory!

Pure glory!

I completed my challenge with twenty-one seconds to go. I had read the minds of twenty-six different dog breeds and I was the winner. The audience went wild. Take that, Wolfgang and Schnitzel! They might be able to make a dozen Dobermans disappear, but could they tell you what flavour ice cream each Doberman was thinking about?

Barbara Barkington-Truffle looked like she was having the time of her life. And I could see Frankie Floofle Toes in the front row – with the look on his face that I imagine TV producers get when they're about to offer a sausage dog his own TV show!

The rest of the cast and crew rushed onto the stage and the Greyhounds of Sound lifted me up off the ground and chanted my name.

'The show's saved!' said Humphrey, clutching his mobile phone. 'The box office phones are going wild!'

'And it's all thanks to Michael!' said Bernadette.

Michael! Michael!

Michael! Michael!

Everyone on stage howled with delight and even Susan smiled at me and said thank you like she meant it. The audience barked in appreciation, and some even leapt off their chairs to chase their tails. There were already some pups queuing up at the side of the stage for my pawtograph.

'Move over Wolfgang and Schnitzel, there's a new show in town!' said Humphrey. 'The Canine Spectacular is here to stay!'

Once everyone had calmed down about how much of a hero I was, Bernadette passed me my sparkly microphone. 'It's time for your winner's speech, Michael,' she said.

I'd almost forgotten! The winner's speech was the final part of the show where the challenge winner got to say a few words while the Greyhounds of Sound were winched down on a floating platform singing a special rendition of 'We Are the Champions'.

I stepped forward.

'Thank you! Thank you!' I said, addressing the crowd. 'I've been waiting for this moment my whole life! The chance to entertain a Hollywoof audience! There's so much I want to say…'

But then the words dried up. Because I realised that something was missing. Something more important than a big speech.

Something large and hairy. The chicken to my chew. The pork to my chop. The squeak to my toy. Stanley Big Dog!

'Wait a minute!' I barked at the audience, dropping my glittery microphone.

I rushed backstage and found Stanley eating a roast chicken ice cream near the costume wardrobe.

'Stanley! You've got to come back on stage!' I barked.

'But I've finished my bit,' replied Stanley, slurping his ice cream. 'This is your bit. The bit at the end where you get a big round of apawse.'

'That's the bit I need you for!' I said.

Stanley Big Dog cocked his head to one side.

'The bit with the apawse – that should be your bit too!' I said.

And I dragged Stanley back onto the stage with me. Because without Stanley, I wouldn't have even been there at all. We took a bow together and the crowd went wild.

The confetti cannon was fired. Greyhounds of Sound burst into song. And I was living the dream, with Stanley Big Dog – the best assistant ever, and my best friend.

Chapter 20
WHO ON EARTH IS STEVE?

Things moved quickly after my outstanding performance at *The Canine Spectacular* finale. Frankie Floofle Toes was bowled over by my talent and offered me my own TV show. And since the TV studio was just round the corner from the Hollywoof Theatre, I could film my TV episodes by day and perform my sell-out theatre show with the rest of the gang by night!

Stanley Big Dog and I were having a blast rehearsing for my new TV show, *An Audience with Michael*. When we weren't rehearsing, we were coming up with ideas for new Michael merchandise. And when we weren't doing either of those things we were basking in the sunshine or eating gourmet pork chops. I was the most famous sausage dog in the world and I was loving it.

One day, Stanley Big Dog and I were at Buttons and Bones approving designs for my new range of Michael waistcoats when Humphrey Huge Dog rushed in with a newspaper. He dropped it at my feet with a look of concern.

'You're not going to like this, Michael!' he said.

And I didn't. The news headline read:

SAUSAGE DOG STEVE TIGHTROPE WALKS ACROSS THE GRAND CANYON! WHILE BALANCING A PEANUT ON HIS NOSE!

There was a picture of a ginger sausage dog puppy posing for pictures surrounded by fans clambering for his pawtograph.

'Word on the street is that Steve might be the NEW most famous sausage dog in the world!' said Humphrey.

'That's impossible!' I barked. 'I'm the most famous sausage dog in the world!'

'That was yesterday,' said Humphrey. 'I believe you're now the second-most famous sausage dog in the world.'

'This is a disaster!' I said.

'Can't we just be second?' said Stanley. 'That sounds OK.'

Humphrey Huge Dog nodded in agreement. 'Yes, I'm not sure that you can beat this pup. He's planning to do the highest bungee jump whilst juggling pork chops. AND it's being live streamed!'

'Ooh, what time?' said Stanley.

'Stanley! We're not watching it,' I barked. 'We have to beat Steve, not become one of his fans!'

'How can you be more famous than that?' said Humphrey. 'You'd have to do something even more extraordinary. It's impossible, Michael!'

My ears pricked up. When you are a world-class talent, things that seem ridiculous to ordinary dogs are exciting opportunities. Tell me I can't do something and I'll want to do it ten times over.

'Stanley, fetch our most fabulous waistcoats, please,' I said. 'We have something spectacular to plan!'

Thank you for reading my book.

You chose this fantastic book by me —
Michael, the Mind-Reading Sausage Dog
— and you have read the whole thing.
This tells me that you are extremely
clever and probably awesomely talented
like myself. So, I give you this advice
as a parting gift...

Remember... There will always be dogs
that don't believe in you. Dogs who say
you're not good enough. That your ears
are too flappy, or your bark
is too squeaky.
But if you have a dream, you can do
anything. All you need is a fabulous
sequinned waistcoat, the knowledge
that you are awesome ... oh, and a large
hairy assistant of course.

MICHAEL

THE STUPENDOUS SUPER-SLEUTH SAUSAGE DOG

Watch out for Michael's next amazing adventure, coming in spring 2024...

When Susan the Chocolate Labrador is dognapped,
Michael and Stanley Big Dog have to turn detective
and face notorious cheese-loving
super villain, Dog X!

Find out more about Michael and Stanley's Amazing Adventures here:

Acknowledgements

A book is never the work of one person alone.

Thank you to all of these people who are infused in every single page.

- Leonie, Becka, Karen, Penny and everyone at Firefly Press and Bounce Marketing
- Alice and Amber
- Lou Kuenzler, plus all my fellow students at Citylit
- Harriet, Hannah, Matilde, Beth and The Longs
- My Mum, Dad and sister, Jo

And of course, thank you to Tim for being such a fantastic illustrator and bringing the dogs of my imagination to life with so much flair.

Environmental statement

At Firefly we care very much about the environment and our responsibility to it.

Many of our stories involve the natural world, our place in it and what we can all do to help it, and us, survive the challenges of the climate emergency. Go to our website **www.fireflypress.co.uk** to find more of our great stories that focus on the environment, like *The Territory, Aubrey and the Terrible Ladybirds, The Song that Sings Us* and *My Name is River*.

As a Wales-based publisher we are also very proud of the beautiful natural places, plants and animals in our country on the western side of Great Britain.

We are always looking at reducing our impact on the environment, including our carbon footprint and the materials we use, and are taking part in UK-wide publishing initiatives to improve this wherever we can.